Breann Malone

THE BERENSTAINS'

B

BOOK

THE BERENSTAINS' B BOOK

A Bright & Early Book

RANDOM HOUSE / NEW YORK

U V W X   5 6 7

Big

brown

Big brown bear

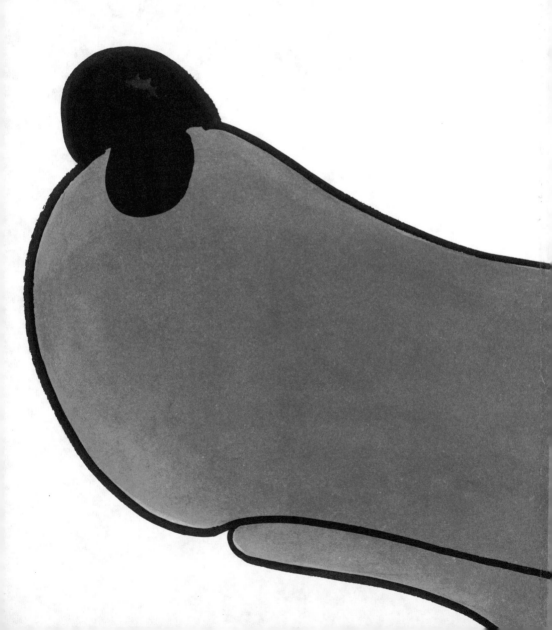

Big brown bear,

blue bull

Big brown bear,

blue bull,

beautiful baboon

Big brown bear,
blue bull,
beautiful baboon
blowing bubbles...

Big brown bear, blue bull,
beautiful baboon
   blowing bubbles
      biking backward...

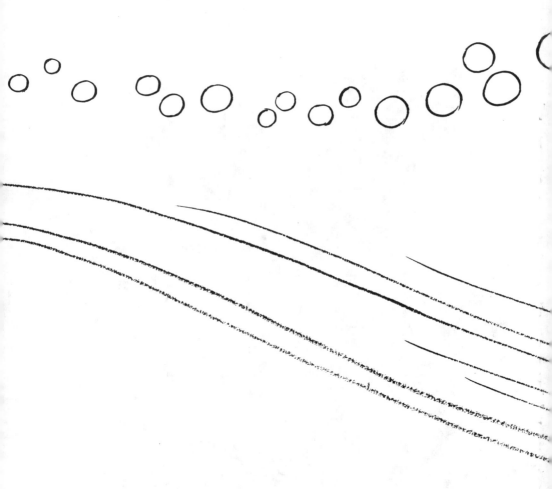

Big brown bear, blue bull,
beautiful baboon
blowing bubbles
biking backward,

bump...

Big brown bear,
blue bull, beautiful baboon
blowing bubbles biking backward,
bump black bug's
banana boxes...

Big brown bear,
blue bull,
beautiful baboon
blowing bubbles
biking backward,
bump black bug's
banana boxes **and**
Billy Bunny's
breadbasket...

Big brown bear,
blue bull,
beautiful
baboon
blowing bubbles
biking backward,
bump
black bug's
banana boxes
and
Billy Bunny's
breadbasket
and...

Brother Bob's

baseball bus...

Big brown bear,
blue bull, beautiful baboon
blowing bubbles biking backward,
bump black bug's banana boxes **and**
Billy Bunny's breadbasket **and**
Brother Bob's baseball bus **and**
Buster Beagle's banjo-
bagpipe-bugle band…

and

that's

what...

broke Baby Bird's balloon.